ASIA

Route of the Bounty

Timor
14 Jun 1789

AUSTRALIA

The mutiny
28 Apr 1789

Pitcairn
Island
15 Jan
1790

Tofua

Tahiti
Arrived
26 Oct 1788
Left
4 Apr 1789

On the morning of 28 April 1789, the most famous mutiny in British naval history took place aboard HMS Bounty. Lieutenant William Bligh and eighteen loyal sailors were cast adrift in a tiny boat by a rebellious crew, led by Fletcher Christian.

This beautifully illustrated book traces the voyage of the Bounty, describes what life was like on an eighteenth century ship and examines the causes of the mutiny.

For Anna

Acknowledgments

The publishers and author would like to thank the staff at the National Maritime Museum who generously gave their time to help with this book, also Andrew Lincoln, and the following for permission to use illustrative material:

G W Lennox 5 top, 25; Mary Evans Picture Library 5 bottom, 26 top; National Maritime Museum title page, 4 (2), 11, 13 (2), 14 (2), 15, 18, 19 (2), 20, 21 (2), 22 (3), 27, back endpaper A top and bottom, back cover: private collection 26 bottom, back endpaper A middle.

Designed by Nick Freestone.

British Library Cataloguing in Publication Data

Lincoln, Margarette
   Mutiny on the Bounty.
   1. Great Britain. Royal Navy. Sailing vessels: Bounty (ship). Mutiny
   I. Title   II. Dillow, John   III. Series
   359.1′334
   ISBN 0-7214-1236-X

First edition

Published by Ladybird Books Ltd Loughborough Leicestershire UK
Ladybird Books Inc Auburn Maine 04210 USA
© LADYBIRD BOOKS LTD MCMLXXXIX

Printed in England

Mutiny on the Bounty

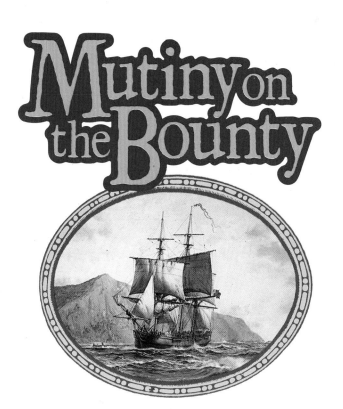

written by MARGARETTE LINCOLN
with illustrations by JOHN DILLOW

Produced in association with the
NATIONAL MARITIME MUSEUM

Ladybird Books

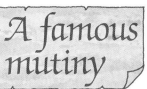

A famous mutiny

The most famous mutiny in British naval history took place on 28 April 1789 aboard HMS *Bounty*. At the centre of the mutiny were two men, the captain of the ship, Lieutenant William Bligh, and Fletcher Christian, who led the crew's rebellion.

◁ *William Bligh. He was 33 when he was given command of the* Bounty.

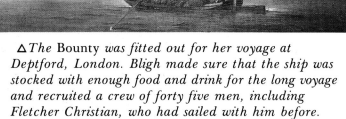

△ *The* Bounty *was fitted out for her voyage at Deptford, London. Bligh made sure that the ship was stocked with enough food and drink for the long voyage and recruited a crew of forty five men, including Fletcher Christian, who had sailed with him before.*

4

The breadfruit plant is the same size as an apple tree. Its fruit, when baked, is similar to bread.

The story began in 1787, when Bligh was given command of the *Bounty*. His job was to sail to Tahiti to collect a cargo of breadfruit plants and take them to the West Indies. The breadfruit was to be used as a cheap food for the slaves who worked on the sugar plantations there.

▷ *Selling a slave in the West Indies.*

The Bounty

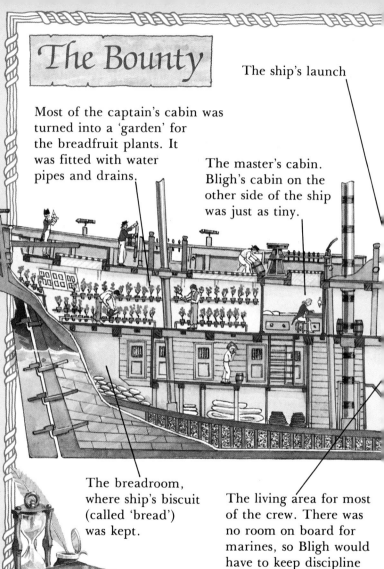

The ship's launch

Most of the captain's cabin was turned into a 'garden' for the breadfruit plants. It was fitted with water pipes and drains.

The master's cabin. Bligh's cabin on the other side of the ship was just as tiny.

The breadroom, where ship's biscuit (called 'bread') was kept.

The living area for most of the crew. There was no room on board for marines, so Bligh would have to keep discipline without their help.

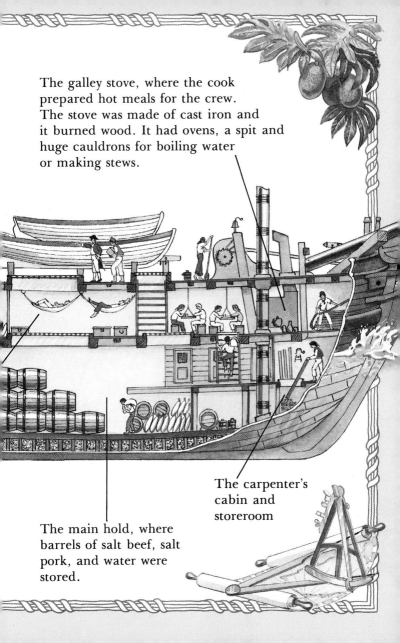

The galley stove, where the cook prepared hot meals for the crew. The stove was made of cast iron and it burned wood. It had ovens, a spit and huge cauldrons for boiling water or making stews.

The carpenter's cabin and storeroom

The main hold, where barrels of salt beef, salt pork, and water were stored.

A ship's crew

▷ A **lieutenant** was one of the junior officers on a ship. When Lieutenant Bligh was given command of the *Bounty*, he was not promoted to the rank of captain. This made it more difficult for him to control his crew.

◁ The **master** was a senior member of the crew. His duties included plotting the ship's position.

▷ Some **master's mates** were training to be masters. Others, like Fletcher Christian, were regarded as future lieutenants and expected to behave like officers.

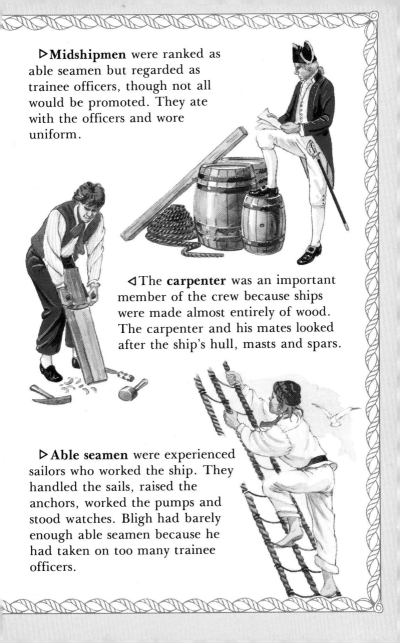

▷**Midshipmen** were ranked as able seamen but regarded as trainee officers, though not all would be promoted. They ate with the officers and wore uniform.

◁The **carpenter** was an important member of the crew because ships were made almost entirely of wood. The carpenter and his mates looked after the ship's hull, masts and spars.

▷**Able seamen** were experienced sailors who worked the ship. They handled the sails, raised the anchors, worked the pumps and stood watches. Bligh had barely enough able seamen because he had taken on too many trainee officers.

The Bounty sets sail

After long delays while Bligh waited for orders from the Admiralty, the *Bounty* finally set sail for Tahiti on 23 December 1787. To give his men more sleep, Bligh introduced a three-watch system. This put men on duty for four hours out of every twelve, instead of the usual four hours out of every eight. Bligh needed a third watch officer and appointed Fletcher Christian. Later, he made Christian acting lieutenant. This favouritism caused jealousy among the crew.

▽ *Bligh kept his men fit on the long voyage by making them dance in the evenings.*

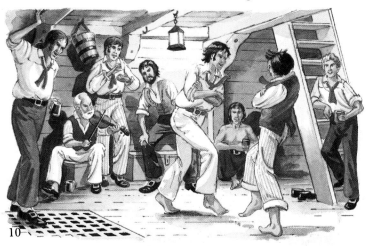

△Sailors were allowed plenty of food but their diet was plain. At sea they ate mostly salted beef or pork and ship's biscuit. A ship would also carry live animals and casks of cheese, butter and dried cod. Fresh fruit and vegetables were available only if the ship put into port. Sailors usually drank rum or beer because their drinking water often went bad.

▽Sailors were allowed 1 lb (464 g) of ship's biscuit a day. It was hard, dry, and full of weevils.

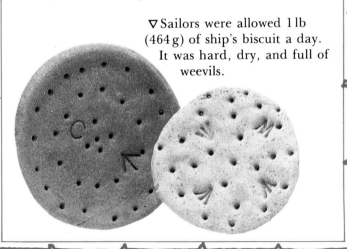

Around the Horn

Three months after leaving England the *Bounty* reached Cape Horn, where it was lashed by gales and heavy seas. After battling against storms for three weeks, Bligh was forced to head back and take the longer, eastwards route to Tahiti, round the Cape of Good Hope.

After months at sea, in an overcrowded ship, the crew became difficult to control.

△ *Because there was such a small number of skilled seamen on the* Bounty, *they had much to do when the weather was stormy.*

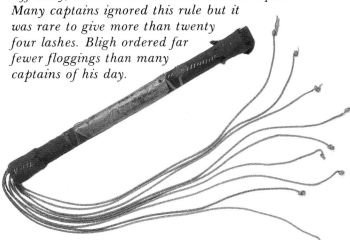

▽*A cat-o'-nine-tails, used for flogging sailors. Officially, twelve lashes was the maximum punishment. Many captains ignored this rule but it was rare to give more than twenty four lashes. Bligh ordered far fewer floggings than many captains of his day.*

Bligh was short-tempered and swore at his men if he thought they weren't working hard enough. By the time they reached Tahiti, many bore grudges against their captain.

▷*An eighteenth century globe used to teach navigation.*

Friendly islanders

Hundreds of islanders rowed out to meet the *Bounty* when it finally reached Tahiti on 26 October 1788. The crew were eager to go ashore after so long at sea but first Bligh made them swear not to tell the islanders why they had come. He did not want the natives to think he had come to steal one of their most important foods. Luckily, Bligh persuaded Tinah, one of the chiefs, that he should send breadfruit plants as a gift to the King of England.

▽ *Tinah, one of the Tahitian chiefs.*

Native canoes off the beautiful island of Tahiti.

△ *Bligh spent hours at ceremonies like this, instead of keeping his men well disciplined.*

Bligh's crew began collecting the plants. This was easier than life at sea, and the sailors grew lazy. Women on Tahiti were friendly and there was plenty of food, so the crew neglected their duties and enjoyed themselves.

▷ *Tahitian children had their bodies tattooed. A sharp tool made of shell or bone was dipped into black liquid. The point was driven into the skin, leaving a black mark. Many of the ship's crew, including Fletcher Christian, were tattooed like this.*

Mutiny at sea

After five months on Tahiti, the *Bounty* left with its cargo of breadfruit. Many of the ship's crew were sad to leave the island. At sea, the men's mood grew worse when Bligh complained that they did not do their work properly.

Countdown to mutiny ~ 28 April 1789

1 Christian and his fellow mutineers drag Bligh from his bunk.

2 They tie Bligh's hands behind his back and haul him to the upper deck.

3 The mutineers argue about what they should do with Bligh.

The crisis came when Bligh accused them of stealing from his supply of coconuts. Fletcher Christian, once a favourite of Bligh, was particularly upset at the captain's insults and decided to desert ship. One of the crew whispered to him that the sailors were ready to mutiny. Christian decided to seize the ship.

4 Bligh and some of his supporters are ordered into the launch. The rest of Bligh's supporters are made to stay on the *Bounty*.

5 The men in the launch beg supplies and navigational tools from their old shipmates.

6 The mutineers threaten to fire on the launch. Bligh gives orders to cut the launch adrift.

The nightmare boat journey

Bligh and eighteen men loyal to him were set adrift with poor supplies of food and drink. As the *Bounty* disappeared into the distance, Bligh must have wondered if he would live to see England again.

▽ *The* Bounty's *launch was only 7 m long and 2 m wide.*

◁ *Each man lived on two ounces (57 g) of bread and a gill (142 ml) of water a day. Bligh made scales out of two coconuts and used lead bullets to weigh out the ration.*

Bligh's later career

After the trial of the mutineers, Bligh's reputation was in ruins. But England was at war with France and he was given command of another ship.

Bligh was involved in other mutinies. In 1797 the whole fleet revolted against pay and conditions.

△ *Bligh's ship, HMS* Glatton, *was badly damaged at Copenhagen.*

He came out of this well and went on to fight bravely in the French wars, taking part in two great battles – Camperdown and Copenhagen. After Copenhagen, Nelson himself praised Bligh's courage.

▷ Some of the things Bligh used on board ship — a pipe, corkscrew, magnifying glass and eyeglass.

Bligh died in 1817. He was a brave and clever man. Today he is unfairly remembered as the monster captain of the *Bounty* who drove his men to mutiny.

◁ Bligh's wife, Elizabeth. She died five years before her husband.

Bligh became Governor of New South Wales, Australia, in 1805. He lived at Government House in Sydney.